P9-DMK-974

Uncle Daddy

To my friend Judy Eggemeier
who knows the power
of writing
+ books!

Ralph Fletcher

Uncle Daddy

by Ralph Fletcher

Henry Holt and Company
New York

Henry Holt and Company, LLC
Publishers since 1866
115 West 18th Street
New York, New York 10011

Henry Holt is a registered trademark of Henry Holt and Company, LLC

Published in Canada by Fitzhenry & Whiteside Ltd.,
195 Allstate Parkway, Markham, Ontario
L3R 4T8.

Library of Congress Cataloging-in-Publication Data
Fletcher, Ralph J.
Uncle Daddy / Ralph Fletcher.
p. cm.
Summary: When his long-absent father suddenly reappears, nine-year-old Rivers struggles with conflicting feelings and reexamines his relationship with the great-uncle who had served as his father.
[1. Fathers and sons—Fiction. 2. Great-uncles—Fiction. 3. Family problems—Fiction. 4. Drug abuse—Fiction.] I. Title.
PZ7.F634 Un 2001 [Fic]—dc21 00-44907

ISBN 0-8050-6663-2
First Edition—2001
Printed in the United States of America on acid-free paper. ∞

1 3 5 7 9 10 8 6 4 2

To my editor
Nina Ignatowicz
who leads me through the fire

Contents

Uncle Daddy

1.

MEMORY BOOK

Uncle Daddy and I are out hiking through the woods. We're surrounded by pine trees so dense the forest seems almost gloomy. But a bit farther the path opens into a sunny little meadow. We have to stop a minute, blinking, letting our eyes get used to the light. He notices something and stops to look at some wild-flowers.

"Trillium," he says, and picks one.

A little farther he bends down again.

"These are jack-in-the-pulpit."

Back home Uncle Daddy takes a book down from a shelf in his room. It's a humongous dictionary, the kind you might see in a library. This monster must weigh at least twenty pounds. It's a foot thick, and it's got two thousand and twenty-three pages in it. Those last twenty-three pages really kill me. I mean, they could've just called it quits at an even two thousand. But no! They just had to give you those extra twenty-three pages, as if you didn't already have more words than any one person could possibly use.

Uncle Daddy opens the dictionary. He flips through the pages until he finds *jack-in-the-pulpit*. He puts the jack-in-the-pulpit blossom into the book, right next to the word. Then he finds the word *trillium* and tucks the yellow blossom into the book, right next to that word.

"Trillium," I say. "That sounds more like a song than a flower."

"Or a radioactive element," Uncle Daddy says, smiling.

I was in first grade the first time I saw Uncle Daddy open the big book. That day he put a salt-water taffy wrapper (he had just taken me to visit a candy factory) next to the word *taffy*.

"Why are you doing that?" I asked him.

"I'm going to use this dictionary like a memory book," he explained. "Someday, when you're all grown up, you'll open this book to look up a word and you'll find this stuff."

Since then I've seen him do the same thing a hundred times. After we go to the circus, he puts one of the ticket stubs next to the word *circus*. A bright autumn leaf goes in the *M*'s, next to the word *maple*. In the past few years he's saved so much stuff in that dictionary that it's pretty lumpy. Now he closes the huge book, hoists it up, and puts it back on the shelf.

"Someday you'll open this book and all these little things will remind you of all the fun we've had together." He smiles at me. "And you'll remember me."

As if I could forget him.

2.
UNCLE DADDY

The first time my friend Taylor came over to my house she was confused about Uncle Daddy.

"Is he your father or your uncle?" she wanted to know.

"Yes," I explained.

The truth is that Uncle Daddy isn't either my father or my uncle. He's actually Mom's uncle. I was three years old when he came to live with us.

Uncle Daddy took care of me. He told me stories, gave me my bath, got me dressed, combed my hair, packed my lunch. He sat through every single one of the dumb holiday shows I did in nursery school, kindergarten, first grade, etc.

I call him Uncle Daddy.

"I had a good life even before I met you," he told me one time. "A great, big hot-fudge sundae. You're the delicious extra scoop that got piled on top."

When I was little he would stand next to me while I brushed my teeth. Brushing your teeth was real important to him.

"You've got to fight the dragon," he told me, and I knew what that meant. He had a strict rule that I had to brush each tooth at least seven times. We counted together—one, two, three, four, five, six, seven—and when I'd done my uppers and lowers, fronts and backs, I'd tilt my head back, give him a toothpasty grin, and demand: "Hand-cup!"

Uncle Daddy would swoop down his big hand, cup it underneath the faucet, fill it with water, and bring it to my mouth. I'd drink two or three cups of water from his hand like that. The water always tasted cool and sweet.

• • •

When I was little I was the world's worst catcher. And I mean the worst! Mom's got videotapes showing me with a glove and a Red Sox hat. Uncle Daddy throws me the ball, and I miss it every time. But he taught me how to catch.

Here's how he did it. He stood in front of me holding a rubber ball. He held the ball so close to my glove it was about one inch away.

"Here you go," he said and threw the ball, dropped it really, into my glove.

"Willie Mays!" he yelled when I caught it. He always called out the names of his favorite players.

Then he moved back a tiny step, so he was holding the ball maybe a foot from my glove. He tossed the ball and I caught it.

"Roberto Clemente!" he called when I caught it again. His face held nothing but pride.

Now back another half-step.

"Carl Yazstremski!" he yelled when I caught it a third time.

The same thing every day. We started real

close together and moved back from there. If I missed one he'd just laugh and throw it again. I got better and better and pretty soon I didn't need to start out so close to him. Pretty soon we were playing catch like any other father and his kid.

3.
MY REAL FATHER

My real father left when I was three years old. The way Mom tells it, he climbed into the car and drove off to get a pizza one summer night, and she never heard from him again. Not a postcard. Not even one phone call.

In her bedroom Mom's got a picture of him, and sometimes I wander in to look at it. In the photo he's a regular-looking guy with droopy brown eyes. He's got the same brown hair as me, and it looks like he's starting to go bald. I'm sitting on his lap in front of a hotel pool, and we both have the same goofy grins.

"What happened?" I've asked Mom a couple

hundred times. "Why did he just leave like that?"

Usually when I ask her she just sighs or rubs her head or closes her eyes and gives me a tired smile.

But sometimes she would say, "He was going through a lot of stuff back then."

Or: "We were just kids."

Or: "I guess he had certain things he needed to work out."

As if that explained anything.

All I know for sure is the fact that when I was three years old he drove out to get a pizza and he never came back.

I've always wondered about that pizza. I mean, whatever happened to it? Did he eat it himself when he went off to wherever he was going?

My friend Taylor used to have a cocker spaniel named Scooter. One night Scooter ran away. That happened a couple of years ago, and Taylor knows he's probably dead but she still keeps looking for him. She can't help it. She checks the woods, the hills, and especially the grassy fields, because that was his favorite place to run.

Same with me. I keep looking for some thirty-five-year-old guy to stop me on the street and start talking to me like we're long-lost friends.

"I'm your father," he'd say. Then he'd smile as if he expected me to start screaming and jumping around like some fool who just found out he'd won the lottery.

"Oh yeah?" I'd shoot back. "For your information I've got a father. So why don't you go back to where you came from?"

Then I'd give him something I've been planning for a long time. I'd wind up and sock him as hard as I could, right in the stomach.

4.

AN UN-BIRTHDAY

I looked at the clock: 2:35. School was almost done, but I was in a bad mood. The classroom felt hot and we were doing math, and Ethan Pierce was annoying me big-time.

"Today is the oneth of June!" Ethan yelled, pointing at the calendar. A few kids giggled. Ethan loved to show off, and when he had an audience he was worse.

"Tomorrow will be the twoth of June!" he proclaimed, making the word sound like *tooth*. The same kids laughed again. I tried to ignore him, but it was hard. He had two ways of talking—loud and louder.

"*Rivers!*" Ethan hissed at me.

"What?"

"How is your super-awesome Uncle Daddy?" he asked.

"Fine," I said.

Uncle Daddy was principal at an elementary school thirty miles away. Ethan's mother had a friend who was a teacher at Uncle Daddy's school.

"You know what my mom's friend told me?" Ethan whispered. "She said your Uncle Daddy sang a song over the loudspeaker."

"Ethan, has the bell rung?" Ms. Vitkevich, our teacher, asked.

"No, ma'am."

"Then turn down the volume," Ms. Vitkevich told him. "Way down."

"Yes, ma'am," he replied.

"Hey, when you come over my house you can meet my Uncle Grandpa!" Ethan whispered to me. "You can meet my Uncle Cousin!"

"Ethan Pierce," Ms. Vitkevich said, standing up. "Didn't I just ask you to lower your voice?"

"Sorry," Ethan said meekly. He bent to his math. A visitor came into the class. When Ethan saw that Ms. Vitkevich was busy he leaned forward and whispered in my ear: "But the person I really, *really* want you to meet is my Uncle Uncle!"

Getting on the bus felt like climbing into a heated oven. A boy opened three little bus windows but that didn't help. Taylor and I sat next to each other, staring out the window.

"Good thing Ms. V. didn't give us much homework," she said, giving me a sly look. "You've got work to do."

I knew she was fishing, and this time it worked.

"Such as . . . ?"

"Such as planning for your party," she said with a smug smile.

My Un-Birthday!

See, I'm one of those lucky kids born on December 25. A Christmas birthday. It sounds pretty cool, but it's not. Ask anybody who's born on Christmas and they'll tell you the truth: you get gypped. Lots of people forget your birthday when it's on that day. Or they give you a combined Christmas-and-birthday gift.

That's how my Un-Birthday got started.

Mom says my real father came up with the idea. Ever since I can remember I've had an Un-Birthday exactly half a year after my real birthday. The Un-Birthday falls on June 25, which is right around the last day of school.

"It's less than four weeks away!" I said to Taylor. "Better be nice," I warned her, "if you want to get invited."

"I'll take my chances," she calmly replied.

Our house was even hotter than the bus. The air conditioning went out a few days ago, and it still wasn't fixed. I found Mom stretched out on the recliner on the back porch, eyes closed, wearing her dark-blue U.S. Mail uniform. She has beautiful blond hair, but today it was plastered against her sweaty neck.

"Hiya, Ma," I said.

"Hellooo," she crooned, keeping her eyes shut. She didn't move her upper body, but her toes wiggled in a kind of greeting. "How was school?"

"Hot."

"It is soooooo hot!" she moaned.

"Don't you have AC in your jeep?"

"I wish." She sighed. "There's a little fan that pulls the hot air from the back of the jeep and blows it onto my face. I was about to faint delivering the mail."

I went into the house, got a clean washcloth, ran it under cold water, squeezed it, folded it, brought it back outside, and put the wet cloth across her forehead.

"Ooooh, thank you," Mom said. "You are a prince."

"You're welcome. Can't we get somebody to fix the AC?"

"The air-conditioning company can't come until sometime next week," she said. "But I just got a brilliant idea. Let's go to a movie tonight. They keep it so cold in there you have to wear a sweater."

"Great!"

Mom took off the cloth and sat up to look at me.

"I need to talk to you." She stopped to take a breath. "I think I want to go out. You know. On a date."

I stared at her.

"Did somebody . . . ask you out?"

"Is that so hard to believe?" she asked. She had just turned thirty-five. She was tall (six feet) and pretty, especially when she smiled, but now she was frowning.

"No, it's a blind date," she explained. "A blind double date. My friend Trish knows this guy. I've never met him but she says he's nice. So Trish and Sam are going out with me and Walker."

"Walker?" I laughed at the name.

"I feel old for a blind date," Mom said. "But I figure: what the heck? Are you sure you're okay with it?"

"Sure, I'm okay," I said. "But, Mom, we have to plan my Un-Birthday."

"My God!" Her eyes snapped open wide. "It's less than a month away!"

"Mom!"

"Okay, okay," she said, laughing. "So let's plan it. What do you have in mind?"

"Uncle Daddy said I can bring four of my friends to his school on a Saturday for a couple of hours." I rubbed my hands together. "He says we can run the school, do anything, play anything we want. *Anything!* It's going to be a blast!"

"Well, he's the principal, isn't he?" Mom said. "How are you going to decide who to invite?"

"I'm still trying to figure that out," I said. "After that I want to come back here and have a party with my whole class. We can play football and have a cookout. Then have a big bonfire on the back lawn, roast marshmallows, tell ghost stories, stuff like that."

"Okay," Mom said, nodding. "Let's just hope the weather is nice. You want to invite the whole class to the party?"

"Yeah."

"Even the girls?"

"Yeah."

"Even Ethan Pierce?" Mom asked.

"Even Ethan." I sighed.

5.
ETHAN PIERCE

It was hot in school. The building was air-conditioned, but in the morning we got a full blast of direct sun through the big windows. Ms. Vitkevich said it was a perfect example of the "greenhouse effect." Maybe so, but all that heat sure made everyone act a little cranky.

Plus, there was Ethan Pierce sitting right smack next to me.

"Your Un-Birthday party is going to be totally Un-Cool!" he hissed in my hair.

Uncle Daddy taught me that when someone makes you mad you should count slowly to ten. I took a deep breath and tried it now: *one, two, three, four, five, six . . .*

"You inviting me to your Un-Birthday?" Ethan asked.

"Un-Fortunately not," I lied. He didn't know I was inviting the whole class. And I was in no big hurry to tell him.

"Aw, pleeeeeeeeeease!" he begged. "I want to come to your Un-Birthday! I want to eat Un-Cake! I want to eat Un–Ice-Cream!"

Eleven, twelve, thirteen, fourteen . . .

"I'll be so Un-Happy if I can't come to your Un-Birthday! It will be so Un-Fair!"

"You are the most annoying kid in this class," I told him.

"Un-True!" Ethan yelled.

"Ethan Pierce." Ms. Vitkevich came and stood right next to his desk. "One more outburst like that and you've got detention. Is that clear?"

"Yes, ma'am," he whimpered.

"Don't *ma'am* me!" she shot back. "Just show a little more respect for the other students in this classroom."

That shut Ethan up for the rest of the morning. But as soon as we went outside for recess he started pestering me again.

"I want to have Un-Fun at your Un-Birthday!"

Ethan cried. "I want to come to your party *so* badly! Please, Rivers!"

Now he actually got down on his knees and pressed his hands together.

"Please!" he begged. "I promise to buy you the best Un-Present in the whole wide world!"

After school I went over to Taylor's house. She and I decided to pull names out of a hat to see which kids would come to play at Uncle Daddy's school. We had a list of all the kids in the class, and she helped me print each kid's name on a separate piece of paper.

"Everyone except me," I reminded her. "And don't do you."

She made a face at me. "Why not?"

"You're already coming," I said. "You're my best friend."

I folded up all the other names and put them into a box. Then I reached in and pulled out a slip of paper. As soon as I read the name I slapped the paper down on the table. Ethan Pierce!

We looked at each other without smiling. The idea popped into my head that I could forget about Ethan and pick three other names. I mean, who would know besides Taylor and me? When I looked at Taylor she had this little smile on her face and I knew she was thinking the exact same thing. But then I got depressed, because I knew we wouldn't. We didn't do things like that. Ethan Pierce was coming, like it or not.

"Oh, brother," I said.

"Keep going," Taylor said, and she offered me the box. I picked Jessie and Carly.

"It's going to be great," Taylor said.

"Yeah," I said, and tried to believe it.

On the day of my Un-Birthday party, Taylor, Jessie, Carly, and Ethan came to my house at two o'clock. We all piled into Uncle Daddy's car. He had the top down on his convertible.

"Can you all fit?" Mom asked.

"Sure thing," Uncle Daddy said. "You guys don't mind sharing seat belts, do you?"

In the front seat I double-buckled with Taylor.

"I can't double-buckle," Ethan Pierce announced. "My parents don't allow me to. They say it's unsafe."

"That's okay," Uncle Daddy said. "There are three seat belts back there."

"Have a great time!" Mom called as we backed out of the driveway.

"We'll try!" Uncle Daddy yelled back. "I don't have any snacks, but we'll try to have at least a little fun!"

Taylor and I laughed. On the floor of the car we could see two bags of chips and pretzels, some cans of soda, and a bag of apples. Pretty soon we were cruising down the street, the wind whipping our hair.

"Too windy?" Uncle Daddy asked us.

"NO!" everybody yelled.

"I used to have tons of hair," Uncle Daddy said. He reached up to rub his big bald head. "But driving around with the top down, well, you can see what happened. The wind blew it away. Be careful that doesn't happen to you!"

Taylor giggled.

"Are you the principal of your school?" Ethan asked. No chance the wind could drown out his voice.

"That's right," Uncle Daddy replied. He took a bag of pretzels and passed it to me.

"What's the worst thing about it?" Ethan yelled from the back seat. Taylor flashed me an annoyed smile, but Uncle Daddy smiled like he'd been expecting the question.

"Discipline," he said. "You know, dealing with the kids who get sent to the office."

"Lots of bad kids, huh?" Ethan asked.

"I've never known a bad kid," Uncle Daddy said. "But I've known plenty of good kids who get in trouble once in a while."

"Do you punish them?" Ethan asked.

"Mostly I just talk to them," Uncle Daddy said.

A truck came up alongside, and the driver waved at us. That got everybody in our car yelling: "Hoo! Hoo!" Ethan let out a scream so loud Uncle Daddy almost swerved off the road.

"Ethan, what are you doing!" I yelled.

Uncle Daddy pulled off the road and shut off the engine. For a moment nobody made a sound.

"Sorry," Ethan said in a tiny voice.

Uncle Daddy turned around and looked straight at Ethan.

"If you ever do that again," he said, "I'm going to cloud up and rain all over you!"

For a second I thought Ethan might start crying, but Uncle Daddy touched him on the knee.

"It's okay," he said slowly. "I know you won't ever do that again in my car. Right?"

Ethan nodded without looking at him.

"Good." Uncle Daddy turned on the engine. Taylor snuck a look at me, and I tried like crazy not to laugh.

That did it. Ethan Pierce didn't make a peep the rest of the way, not even when our car pulled into the empty parking lot of the Frances Bellamy Elementary School.

6.

SATURDAY SCHOOL

We started scrambling out of the car, but Uncle Daddy held up his hand.

"Wait a sec," he said. His face looked real serious. "This is Saturday school. Let's lay down some ground rules before we go inside."

Everyone looked at him.

"Rule Number One," he said, looking straight at Ethan Pierce. "NO SOFT VOICES! If I hear any whispering or low voices you're going to be in serious trouble with me."

Carly giggled.

"Rule Number Two!" Uncle Daddy said. "ABSOLUTELY NO WALKING IN THE HALLS!"

"But," Ethan sputtered, "I mean, how, what—"

"In honor of Rivers' Un-Birthday," Uncle Daddy said, "I am giving you free run of my school."

"Did you tell the janitors?" I asked.

"I explained everything to the custodians," he said, nodding. "They know you're going to be running around the school. In the gym you can play with whatever you want, so long as you put everything back. Okay?"

We all nodded, grinning at each other.

"Don't do anything stupid," Uncle Daddy said. "Be safe. And have a blast!"

We burst into the school. The moment we got inside the front doors we started racing down the halls.

"Let's go to the gym!" I yelled.

"Whoo!" the other kids whooped and raced after me. There is no possible way to explain how much I loved the sounds our feet made pounding down those hallways. I mean, all you hear in school is "Walk, don't run," "No running in the halls," "Stay in line." What a terrific feeling to be tearing down the hall, running full-speed, with the stale school air rushing past your face, and all the time knowing *nobody's going to stop you, nobody is going to say a thing about it*. In the gym I ran straight to the equipment closet and yanked open the doors.

"C'mon, you guys!" I cried.

"How many should we bring out?" Taylor asked.

"All of them!" Jessie yelled.

There were about a hundred balls in the closet—bouncy red balls, basketballs, footballs—and we pulled out every one. First we played a game of basketball where each one of us went to a corner of the gym and started shooting. The game was to see who could hit the most shots in two minutes. Then we rolled the basketballs to the side and made up a wild game—half dodgeball, half war—with the bouncy red balls. Jessie pelted me twice on the leg, and he threw the balls so hard they left red spots, but I didn't care.

When we got tired of the gym, we picked up the balls and sprinted to the Main Office.

"How are you doing?" Uncle Daddy asked.

"Great!" I told him.

He made a serious face at Carly.

"You're not walking in the halls, are you?" he asked.

"No, sir," she told him.

"Good." He nodded. "I expect you to follow the rules around here."

"Can we ring the bells?" I asked him.

"Be my guest." He pointed at a panel of switches beside his desk.

"Lemme be first!" Ethan cried. "Please!"

I let him ring the bell. It was so loud it made us all jump.

"School has begun!" Ethan shouted in a funny deep voice. "The students are all hard at work on their studies. But, since I HAVE THE POWER, I have decided that today school will only last one minute!"

He pressed a second button. The loud bell for dismissal.

"Thank you, thank you!" Ethan said, holding up his fists like a boxer who's just won the world championship.

"My turn!" Jessie cried. We all took a turn making the bells ring.

"Hey, can I push that one?" Ethan asked, pointing at another button. Underneath it said: FIRE ALARM.

"That's the only one you *can't* push," Uncle Daddy said. "That one rings in the fire station."

"Oh," Ethan said.

We played in the Main Office for a long time. Uncle Daddy let us use the copy machines, and we had an absolute riot copying our hands, elbows, and ears. Taylor closed her eyes and made a copy of her face.

After that we played hide-and-go-seek. The rules were simple: you could hide anywhere in the school but you couldn't go outside. We split into two teams. While Taylor and I counted to a hundred, the others ran off to hide. After we finished counting, we tiptoed up to the second floor. At the top of the stairs we looked down the long hallways. Totally quiet.

"Let's split up," I whispered.

"No, let's stay together," Taylor said. "It's spooky up here!"

At the first classroom we slowly opened the door. The room was dark. Something moved, and we both jumped.

"Ah!"

But it was just a guinea pig moving in its cage. Taylor pointed to the closet at the back of the room. I opened the door, expecting to see one of the kids jump out at me. But no one did.

The same thing happened in the next classroom, and the next one after that. Finally we decided to split up. Taylor searched the library, and I checked out the locker rooms.

We couldn't find them. They had vanished.

"I've got an idea," I said, and started sprinting back to the Main Office. Uncle Daddy wasn't in his office, but there was a microphone on his desk. I switched the button to "ON" and began speaking into the microphone. I could hear my voice being carried all over the school.

"MAY I HAVE YOUR ATTENTION, PLEASE! MAY I HAVE YOUR ATTENTION, PLEASE! THIS MESSAGE IS FOR ETHAN PIERCE, JESSIE ROSEN, AND CARLY REED. THESE THREE STUDENTS ARE IN TROUBLE,

SERIOUS TROUBLE. JESSIE, CARLY, AND ETHAN, YOU HAVE CHEATED DURING A GAME OF HIDE-AND-GO-SEEK. FOR THIS YOU THREE DORKS WILL BE PUNISHED."

I paused to clear my throat. Taylor was cracking up. With my hand over the mike, I asked her: "How does it sound?"

"Great!" she said. Now I started yelling into the microphone like the wizard in *The Wizard of Oz*.

"DO YOU UNDERSTAND ME? YOU MISERABLE WORMS! YOU SLITHERING TOADS! HOW DARE YOU BREAK THE RULES IN MY SCHOOL! YOU ARE EVIL! YOU ARE ROTTEN! AND YOU WILL PAY FOR YOUR CRIMES! NO DOUBT YOU ARE WONDERING WHAT YOUR PUNISHMENT WILL BE. WELL, I WILL TELL YOU. YOUR PUNISHMENT IS DETENTION FOR THE NEXT TWO YEARS! DO YOU HEAR ME? REPORT TO THE OFFICE IMMEDIATELY, IF NOT SOONER! IF YOU DO NOT REPORT TO THE OFFICE IN THE NEXT TWO MINUTES I WILL ADD FIVE MORE YEARS ONTO YOUR DETENTION!"

Taylor was laughing so hard she was holding her stomach. We heard a loud noise and saw

Ethan, Jessie, and Carly racing toward the Main Office, laughing and whooping at the top of their lungs.

"*Losers!*" Ethan screamed. "We were in the All-Purpose Room the whole time!"

7.
BLIND DATE

In the back yard we had twenty-one kids sitting around a blazing bonfire. Taylor's mother was there, too, to supervise. A breeze sprang up, kicking bouquets of sparks into the night.

"Hey, we're out of marshmallows!" Jessie yelled.

"Yeah," Taylor said, "because you're toasting ten at a time!"

"I am not!"

"I'll go get the other bag," I said.

"Hurry up!" Ethan said. "I'm going to tell the bloodiest ghost story you ever heard."

"*Ooooh,*" Taylor said. "Am I supposed to be scared?"

I found Mom in the kitchen pouring soda into paper cups.

"How's it going out there?" she asked.

"Good. We need the other bag of marshmallows."

"Here you go." She tossed it to me.

"Where's Uncle Daddy?" I asked.

"He was tired," she said. "I think he went to bed."

Just then I heard what sounded like a car door in front of the house. I walked to the living room and peeked through the window. In the driveway there was a car I'd never seen before, an old-fashioned Volkswagen Beetle, and a man was getting out of it.

"Someone's here," I told Mom.

"Must be Walker," she said. "He said he might stop over."

"Walker?"

"You know," Mom said. "The man I had a date with."

"The Blind Date!" I peered out the window. On the darkened driveway I could see that he was wearing a jacket and tie, and carrying something in his hands. "Hey, Mom, looks like he brought me a present. A big one."

"Show him in," she called from the kitchen.

"He's dressed like he's going to church!" I told her. "He's wearing a tie and everything."

"Remember your manners," Mom said. "Make nice."

I went to the door and watched him climb the steps. It's hard not to check out a guy who your mother had a date with. He had a regular kind of face, dark eyebrows, and not too much hair. The guy looked a little nervous. He smiled at me through the front screen door. I opened the door to let him in. He used both hands to carry the present inside and into the hallway.

"Hi," I said, offering him my hand. "I'm . . ."

"I know who you are," he said. He took my hand and held on tight. Then he did a very strange thing. He put the present on the coffee table, put his hands on my shoulders, and stared intently into my eyes.

"It's me, Rivers." He spoke in a soft voice. "Your father. I've come back."

8.

UNSPEAKABLE FOOL

I thought I'd never see him again. I figured him for a goner, possibly dead, definitely dead to me, but there he was, actually standing in our living room. He looked uncomfortable in that gray suit jacket and sky-blue tie.

A thousand times I had imagined exactly what I'd say to him if he ever did show up, one thing meaner than the next. I'd rehearsed it in my head over and over until I could clearly picture the whole thing, right up to the part where I balled up my fists and slugged him in the stomach. Then he would double over, gasping for breath, and I'd push him outside and double-lock the door.

I had planned for this moment, sure, but I'd never imagined it would really come, and now all I could do was stand there, mouth open, staring up like an idiot.

Mom walked into the room and swore. Cursed. I had never heard Mom curse like that.

"Hello, Ana," he said in a soft voice.

"Nelson." She said the word carefully, like a person walking on ice that might break any second. He looked at her and nodded.

"I can't believe it," she said.

"I know, I know," he said. He reached up and fiddled with the knot of his tie. His cheeks were kind of shiny, the way Uncle Daddy's cheeks look after he shaves.

"The house looks . . . good," he said, glancing around at the curtains and ceiling. I could feel Mom looking over at me, trying to catch my eye, but I couldn't keep my eyes off him. He started talking in a voice so low I had to strain to hear him. I listened, more to the sound of his voice than to what those words might mean, but I listened hard.

"I've been wanting to come back for such a long time." He looked at me and smiled. "Your

Un-Birthday just seemed like the right day to do it."

Mom glared at him. He looked at her and cleared his throat.

"I guess I should say the obvious," he said. "I've been an unspeakable fool."

Then why don't you stop talking? I felt like saying. Now that the shock had faded a little, I could feel myself getting mad. The thought hit me that it still might not be too late to slug him in the stomach.

The man looked at me, studying my face.

"Just look at you! My God, how you've grown!" He turned to Mom. "He's got my chin. Got my eyes, too."

I thought: *I don't want anything of yours. Nothing.*

"Look, Rivers, I brought your Un-Birthday present."

So maybe he was the one who started the whole Un-Birthday idea in the first place. He set the present in front of me. When I didn't move he knelt down and ripped it open himself.

"It's a toolbox, a nice sturdy one. I'm good at fixing things, and I can teach you, too, if you want." He opened the toolbox. "You've got a hammer, two kinds of wrenches, measuring tape, a place for nails and screws. Believe me, you don't want all that little stuff spilling all over the place. Look at this. Three kinds of pliers! You won't believe the stuff you can do with a set of needlenose pliers like this."

He looked up at me hopefully, smiling, but I didn't smile back. I didn't know how to feel.

"I've missed you so much," he said.

"You picked a funny way of showing it," Mom said. She started to say more, but right at that moment Taylor came into the living room.

"You're missing Ethan's ghost story," she said to me. She saw my father standing in the middle of the room and whispered to me: "Who's that?"

"A ghost," Mom said. Her voice sounded funny, like it was somebody else talking. "A real live come-back-from-the-dead kind of ghost."

"Very funny," he said, standing.

"I'm not trying to be funny," Mom said in that zombie voice. "I'm dead serious. And I think you better leave now, ghost."

He looked like he was ready for that.

"All right, Ana." He touched me on the arm. "Happy Un-Birthday, Rivers."

He walked out the front door. I don't know why but I walked out behind him. Taylor followed behind me.

"What kind of car is that?" she asked him.

He stopped, turned, and smiled at me, as if I had asked the question.

"You interested in cars?" he asked hopefully.

"No," I told him.

"It's a VW Bug," he said, getting into the car. He looked at me. "I'll come by tomorrow," he said, as he slowly backed his car out of the driveway.

"Who was that guy?" Taylor asked.

"My father," I said.

She took a sharp breath and looked at me. "Really?"

I hated him so much at that moment. More than anything in the world I wanted him to leave and never come back. Ever! But when I tried to swallow, I felt a lump in my throat as I watched him drive away.

9.
THE NEW WORLD

When I went back inside, Mom was standing in the same place. She hadn't moved.

"We'll talk about this later," she said. "Let's not spoil the party. We've still got cake. And you've got those presents to open."

I just looked at her.

"Don't forget these," Mom said, and tossed me the bag of marshmallows.

An hour later my last friend finally left. I was sitting in the kitchen with Mom when Uncle Daddy walked into the room. "Sorry I pooped out on your party," he mumbled.

Both Mom and I just sat there staring at the table.

"I heard you had an unexpected guest," Uncle Daddy said.

"You heard?" Mom asked. Uncle Daddy nodded.

"I decided to stay out of it," he said.

Mom got up, went to the coffeemaker, and poured two cups of coffee. "Yes, he's back. Can you believe it?"

She stared at me and I stared back.

"Well, what happened?" Uncle Daddy wanted to know.

"Rivers?" Mom nudged me.

"He brought me a present," I said. "It's a toolbox with a bunch of tools. He said some stuff about how sorry he was, and then he left. Mom made him."

"Good," Uncle Daddy said. He sipped his coffee.

"What is he doing here, is what I want to know," Mom said.

"That's the question," Uncle Daddy agreed. "Did you ask him?"

Mom shook her head.

"I was in shock." She spoke in a near whisper.

"You're being awful quiet," Uncle Daddy said to me.

"Can he make me go live with him?" I asked. My voice sounded high and panicky, but I didn't care.

"No," Uncle Daddy said. He squeezed my arm, hard.

"Uncle Daddy and I are your family," Mom said. "Nothing has to change, unless you want it to."

"You have a right to see him," Uncle Daddy said with a little shrug. "If that's what you want."

Mom nodded. "He said he was coming to see you tomorrow. You feel okay about that?"

"I don't know."

She got up to pour herself another cup of coffee.

"What do you think?" she asked Uncle Daddy.

"Don't ask," he said, looking straight at her. "You don't want to know."

Mom shot me a quick look.

"Yes, I do," she said.

"No, you don't," he replied.

I went outside with Uncle Daddy to douse the bonfire. Without the fire the back yard was so dark you couldn't see a foot in front of your face. I saw sparks over by the vegetable garden.

"Look, fireflies!" I pointed. "I used to be scared of them, remember? I thought they'd burn my fingers."

"I remember," he said with a soft laugh. He nudged me in the ribs. "Took me all summer to convince you that you wouldn't get electrocuted if you touched one."

In the darkness I reached out and found his big hand. I gave it a little squeeze, and he squeezed back.

I got into bed, but so many thoughts and questions crowded my head I couldn't sleep.

Why had he come back?

Was he going to stay?

What had he been doing for the past six years?

Who was he, anyway?

I got up and stood by the window. The sky was jammed with stars, and those tiny lights made me remember all the nights I lay in bed counting stars and wondering about my father, where he was, why he left me.

When I thought about what happened when he left, I imagined myself as another person. In my mind I can get a real clear picture of that kid. He hears his father say: *I'll go pick up the pizza.* The boy goes to the window and has to lift up onto his tiptoes to watch his father drive away. Then he sits on the kitchen floor to wait.

FORGET IT! I want to scream at that kid. FIND SOMETHING ELSE TO EAT! HE'S NEVER COMING BACK!

10.

TALK, TALK, TALK

My father showed up at noon. I was sitting in the living room when I heard his VW Bug pull into the driveway. He climbed out, wearing sandals, jeans, and a Boston Celtics T-shirt. He had a little piece of tissue under his chin, like he'd cut himself shaving. I opened the door and stepped outside.

"Hey," he said with a little smile. "Want to go for a drive?"

Just then I heard Uncle Daddy's voice behind me.

"Hello, Nelson."

"Hi, Dan," my father said. There was a

funny smile frozen on my father's face. Uncle Daddy's face looked serious. The two men shook hands. The door opened again and Mom came out.

"Hello, Ana," my father said. He looked at the house. "The place looks real good."

"We had it painted last summer," she said. "Replaced all the drainpipes."

"Nice," he said. He motioned over at me. "I thought I'd take Rivers for a drive."

"Just like that, huh?" She folded her arms.

"Just like what?" my father asked.

I wasn't even sure I wanted to go with my father—I was pretty sure I *didn't* want to—but I stood there checking out the looks on people's faces. Mom: mad. Uncle Daddy: solemn. My father: uneasy.

"You've been gone for over six years, Nelson!" Mom spoke in a high voice, and her face was red. "I mean, do you really expect to just show up and drive off to God-knows-where with my son?"

"Our son," he reminded her.

"We need to talk," she said. And with that she

turned and went inside. My father went into the house behind her.

"So what happens now?" I asked Uncle Daddy.

"They talk," he said, taking a seat on the front steps beside me.

"And then . . . ?"

He shrugged and said in a whisper: "Your mom and I hatched a secret plan. See, I'm going to sneak into his car and plant a special high-tech electronic homing device that will allow us to track him if he decides to drive off with you to Timbuktu."

I stared at him.

"Joke, Rivers," he said. "You know, like: ha, ha, ha."

"It's not funny," I said.

"I know."

"Sometimes grown-ups really drive me crazy."

"There's a fourth-grade boy in my school," Uncle Daddy said. "He calls me and the teachers g-r-o-*a*-n–ups because we make him groan."

"Groan-ups," I said with a little laugh. "Hey, that's pretty good."

"C'mon." Uncle Daddy picked up the basketball. "I'll play you a game of horse."

A half hour later my father and mother came outside.

"Rivers," she said. "Your father would like to spend a little time with you. Is that all right?"

I shrugged and sneaked a peek at Uncle Daddy. He gave a little nod of his head.

"I'll take that as a maybe-sort-of-possibly-yes," my father said.

"One hour," Mom said.

"Okay, then," my father said. "Good to see you again, Dan."

Uncle Daddy did not look at him.

I climbed into the car. My father backed out of the driveway. Mom and Uncle Daddy watched us from the front steps. My father put the car into gear, and when it sped up, my heart sped up, too. I remembered a movie I saw on TV about a father who comes back after being away a long time and kidnaps his son. The mother has to contact the FBI to try to get him back.

"Where are we going?" I asked.

"Not far," he said. A little while later he turned into a street. It didn't look much different from the neighborhood where I lived, except there were apartments instead of houses. He slowed the car and turned into one of the driveways.

"I want to show you something," he said.

I followed him up a stairway and waited while he unlocked the door. We stepped into a kitchen.

"This is where I live."

On the other side of the kitchen there was a small living room with a couch, coffee table, and TV. Three boxes were stacked against the wall.

"I moved in five days ago," he said. "Took me a few days to get up the nerve to go over to the house. Still got some unpacking to do. You thirsty? How about a cold soda?"

I shook my head. Only my eyes were thirsty, drinking in everything—magazines, a roll of silver duct tape on top of a small stack of mail, a tape measure on the counter. I pulled the tape out a few inches.

"That's from work," he said.

I looked at him.

"I'm an electrician," he said. "It's a good skill to have. I've already got a job about four miles from here."

I nodded, running my hands over the countertop. I was thinking: *This is my father's toaster. That's where my father makes his coffee. That's my father's table.*

"That's a pull-out sofa," he was saying, "for when you come and stay overnight. I'm hoping you will. Make yourself right at home. I'm going to use the bathroom."

I walked down the hallway and into the bedroom. On top of his dresser there was a photo of me and him. I picked it up. It was the same picture I had, the one with both of us grinning by a hotel pool.

I felt him at the doorway, looking at me.

"Can we go now?" I asked, putting the picture back on his dresser.

"Sure thing," he said.

"You like ice cream?" he asked, pulling out of the driveway.

"Yeah." *Who doesn't like ice cream?*

"There's a place not too far from here," he said. "I thought we might go there."

"Okay."

"You must be feeling good now that school's almost over. How many more days do you have?"

"Two," I said, staring straight ahead. I was back to being mad again, real mad. I wasn't going to punch him in the gut, but I wasn't going to say much, either. One-word answers—*yeah, okay, fine, maybe, sometimes*—that's all he'd get from me.

We drove to the ice-cream shop without another word. We got a table and the first thing I saw was a bunch of my friends, including Ethan Pierce, sitting together. When Ethan saw me, he puffed out his cheeks, crossed his eyes, and started waving like a wild man.

"Friends of yours?" my father asked.

"Sort of," I said. That was two words! I picked up the menu. He smiled and leaned toward me.

"When you were little," he said, "you always made me cut your ice cream into little pieces. If

I didn't cut it up, you wouldn't eat it. Remember that?"

"Nope." I studied the menu.

"What's your favorite flavor?" he asked.

"Vanilla," I lied. I hate vanilla. I go for Double Dark Chocolate Fudge Decadence.

"Vanilla!" he practically shouted.

Ethan gave me a surprised look and shook his head. A moment later his grinning face appeared at our table.

"Hi!" He beamed at my father and stuck out his hand. "I'm Ethan Pierce!"

"Nice to meet you," my father said, shaking hands. "I'm Nelson White. I'm Rivers' father."

"Cool," Ethan said. "I'm Rivers' best friend, only he doesn't know it yet."

I snorted in disgust.

"Well, nice to meet you," Ethan said. He bowed and went back to his table.

"Friendly boy, isn't he?" my father said.

"No," I replied.

The waitress took our orders. Since I was such a big fan of vanilla all of a sudden, I had to order a vanilla cone. Then I hunkered down for the long wait.

"Your favorite flavor is vanilla," he said in a low voice. "I should know that. I should know that."

I said nothing.

"Talk to me, Rivers," he said, leaning forward.

I sipped ice water so cold it hurt my teeth.

"Say *some*thing," he said. "What are you thinking?"

I was thinking of that movie about the father who comes back and kidnaps the son. There's a scene where the mother calls the father a "deadbeat dad." My father left when I was three. And now he was chumming up like we were best buds. I picked up the metal spoon and it was all I could do not to bend it in half.

"I haven't seen you smile once," he said, trying to make eye contact. "Rivers?"

Finally I looked at him.

"What?" I demanded.

"What are you thinking?"

"I was wondering about that pizza," I said in a low voice.

He looked puzzled.

"The pizza," I explained. Now that I'd broken my one-word rule I figured I might as well keep on going. "You know, the pizza you went out to get that night when you left six years ago."

He tilted his head back and closed his eyes.

"You remember that?" he asked after a moment.

I nodded. "I've always wondered what happened to that pizza. Did you just leave it there? Did you eat it yourself? Did you give it to some homeless people? What?"

"I picked it up," he whispered, not looking at me now. "Then I got in the car and started driving."

The waitress came over and refilled our glasses.

"You ate our pizza on the way?" I asked in amazement.

"Some of it," he said. "I was hungry."

"I was hungry, too," I hissed at him. "We kept looking out the window. I kept asking Mom where you were, and Mom kept telling me: *Any minute now. Any minute.*"

"You don't understand," he whispered.

"You're right, I don't." I stood up and ran. I wanted to be just about anywhere on earth but sitting with him.

"Hey, Rivers!" Ethan yelled, but I ignored him and headed toward the door. My father rushed after me.

"Rivers!" he yelled. "Please! You've got to let me explain."

I ran out of the parking lot onto the sidewalk.

"Wait!" he called. "I'll drive you home!"

"No way!" I yelled. I felt the wind blowing past my face and it felt so good I ran faster. I wanted to keep running like that, faster and faster, and never stop.

11.
LIVING IN LIMBO

When I got home I found Uncle Daddy weeding tomato plants in the back yard. He stood, holding his hands in front of him. They were filthy right up to the elbows.

"That was quick," he said, wiping sweat off his nose with the back of his wrist. "So how did it go?"

"Terrible," I said.

I went into the kitchen and Uncle Daddy followed me inside. He washed his hands in the sink. Then he took a coffee cup, filled it with ice cubes, and poured hot coffee over the ice. The cubes made a loud crackling sound.

"Where did you go?" he asked, sitting down at the table with me.

"He took me to see where he lives," I said. "It's an apartment on the other side of the mall. Then he took me for ice cream."

"You want to talk about it?" he asked.

"No."

Uncle Daddy raised his eyebrows and sipped his coffee.

"When he showed up yesterday I thought maybe he was like one of those tumbleweeds," Uncle Daddy said. "You know, just sort of blowing through. But if he's got an apartment it looks like he's going to be around for a while."

I nodded.

"He said he's got a job. He's an electrician."

Uncle Daddy put his hand on my shoulder.

"So how do you feel about all this?"

"Weird," I said. It's one of my favorite words, but it didn't even begin to explain how scrambled up I felt inside.

I went over to Jessie's house for a baseball game. When Ethan Pierce saw me he gave me a funny look.

"Hey, that guy at the ice-cream store?" he asked. "That your real daddy?"

"Yeah, what about it?" I asked.

"But what about Uncle Daddy?" Ethan said. "I mean, now you've got, like, two fathers. Right?"

I stared at him.

"What if, like, they had a boxing match in your living room!" he said. He started dancing around, throwing punches into the air. "Wouldn't that be totally cool?"

"C'mon," I said, trying not to get mad. "Let's choose teams!"

"Or how about if they had, like, a duel!" Ethan said. "You know, like in the old days. They each get a pistol, right? They stand back to back and they count off ten paces, then they turn around and—BLAM! When the smoke clears, whichever guy is left standing, well, he gets to be your father. That would be so awesome!"

"You are really twisted, you know that?" I asked.

"Thank you!" Ethan beamed.

• • •

When I came into our house I could hear voices coming from the kitchen. I went in and saw them. My father. And Mom. She looked like she'd been crying. They kept talking as if I wasn't there.

"I deliver letters," she said softly. "About twenty thousand letters a year. You were gone over six years, and in all the bags of mail I delivered I never saw a single letter from you. Not even *one.*"

"I know," he said in the same soft tone.

"You *don't* know," Mom said, shaking her head. "You left me with a toddler who kept asking for Daddy, and what was I supposed to tell him?" They turned to look at me. "I didn't know if you were dead or alive. We were living in limbo."

He sighed and rubbed his face.

"Remember last year?" Mom asked me. "That Banana Splits program?"

Of course I remembered. My school had a special program for third-grade kids whose parents were split up. They met once a week with the school counselor to talk about divorce and stuff. At the end of the year the kids had an ice-cream party with banana splits. Mom asked me if I wanted to go, but I wasn't sure if I should, since we didn't know if my father was gone forever or what.

"Banana splits?" my father asked.

Right then Uncle Daddy walked into the kitchen from the garage. He approached the table. Everybody froze.

"What are you doing here?" he asked, glaring at my father.

My father looked confused. He glanced over at Mom.

"We were trying to talk," she said in a tired voice.

My father stood up. I could see how much taller he was than Uncle Daddy.

"You want me to leave?" my father asked.

"You could say that," Uncle Daddy retorted, his lips squeezed together so tight they were almost white. He clenched his fists, and my heart started hammering. I was scared they were going to fight.

"You don't like me much, do you?" my father asked.

Uncle Daddy just stared.

"Maybe we—" Mom started to say, but my father raised his hand.

"Hold it," he said to her. He looked back at Uncle Daddy. "Go ahead, give it to me straight."

"You abandoned your family," Uncle Daddy said, jabbing his finger at my father. "In my book there's nothing lower than that. Nothing."

My father let out a breath. He looked around at us: Uncle Daddy, Mom, me.

"I guess that's my exit line, huh?" he said. He nodded. "Okay, I'll leave. Everybody hates me, and maybe I deserve that. But I'm not going to run away again." He looked at me, and his eyes were shining. "You're my kid, Rivers. You're the only kid I've got."

He walked out through the back door, and he left it wide open behind him.

12.
THE HANDYMAN

On the last day of school Ms. Vitkevich collected our textbooks and handed out summer reading lists. Ethan Pierce had somehow managed to smuggle two helium balloons into class.

"Hope you have a wa-wa-wacky summer!" he said in a strange, high voice. The class looked over at Ms. Vitkevich, expecting her to do something.

"I give up," she said with a tired smile. "It's the last day of school. Go right ahead, Ethan."

Ethan Pierce thrust his fist triumphantly into the air. "Earthlings!" he chortled in that weird new voice. "Follow me! I am your new leader!"

"That's what you think," I muttered.

I sat next to Taylor on the way home. All the kids were laughing, singing, cracking jokes.

"We did it," Taylor said. "Do you realize we are technically fifth-graders?"

"Yeah," I said.

"You're awful quiet," she said. "Hey, school's over! No more teachers, no more books . . ."

"I know," I said. Summer has always been my favorite season, but already this summer felt different. I didn't know what to expect.

That afternoon my father showed up at 3:35. He was wearing old jeans and a dirty T-shirt. He carried his toolbox into the house and stood there in the middle of the living room. "Anybody home?"

I knew he meant Uncle Daddy, so I shook my head.

"How's school?" he asked.

"Today was our last day," I said. "I'm a fifth-grader now."

"Congratulations." He grinned.

"How come you're not at work?"

"My shift goes from seven to three," he

explained. "I'm going to see if I can fix this air conditioner."

"How did you know it was broken?" I asked him.

"It's not exactly cool in here," he said, smiling. "You feel like giving me a hand?"

"Well, I'm sort of busy," I told him.

"Suit yourself," he said, and he went to work. I stood there for a moment watching him open his toolbox, and then I went into my bedroom to read comics. Fifteen minutes later I heard a knock on my door. It was him.

"I need a favor," he said. "Mind if I borrow the needlenose pliers I gave you? I forgot mine."

"Well, I guess," I said.

I gave him the pliers, and he went back to work. A little while later I went into the kitchen to get a snack, and I could feel cold air blowing from the living room. I found him in the front hallway.

"What are you doing now?" I asked.

"Doorbell," he said. "Look at this wiring! Can you believe this? It's amazing it didn't start a fire."

After he fixed the doorbell, he replaced a board on the front steps that had rotted out. Then he tightened the loose handle on the refrigerator.

"There's a bunch more to be done but I'm beat," he said. "See you later." He handed back my pliers and left.

The house was nice and cool by the time Uncle Daddy and Mom got home, but they weren't happy about it.

"Who does he think he is?" Uncle Daddy said. "He's got no business coming in here like that without permission."

I could feel them looking at me. "Hey, it's not my fault, okay?" I yelled.

"Of course it's not!" Mom said. She and Uncle Daddy looked at each other.

"Then how come everybody's getting mad at me?" I demanded. "I mean, what was I supposed to do, lock all the doors? Call the police? What?"

"Rivers, it's all right," Mom said. She touched my arm. "It's all right, okay?"

"I didn't know what to do," I said, softer now. I was close to crying.

"We're not mad at you," Uncle Daddy said.

"Right," Mom said, still touching me. "But from now on, he calls before he comes over here."

"Right," Uncle Daddy said. "And if we need something fixed around here, well, I'll pay someone to do it."

"Amen," she said. "I don't need any more fixing from him."

The next day was Mom's day off. She and I were both home when the phone rang.

"Hi, Rivers." It was him.

"Hi."

"Your mother called," he said. "Guess I won't be doing any more repair work around there for a while." There was a pause. "Sorry if I made you uncomfortable or anything."

"It's okay," I said.

"You're playing baseball tonight, right?" he asked. "That's what your mother said."

"Yeah."

"Maybe I'll stop by," he said.

After I hung up, Mom came into the kitchen.

"It was him," I said.

"What did he say?"

"He might come to my game tonight."

"I'll tell you a little secret, Rivers." Mom gave me a straight look. "I don't trust that man. Not after what happened."

"Yeah," I said. "I don't either."

"We'll just have to see."

That night Uncle Daddy and Mom took their usual seats in the bleachers by the first-base line. I led off the second inning. I walked up to the plate and looked over to the bleachers on the third-base side. There he was. My father. Sitting by himself. It wasn't a hot night, but suddenly my palms felt sweaty when I squeezed the bat.

The pitcher wound up and threw a change-up that was supposed to fool me, except I was ready for it. I swung and hit a line drive over the second baseman. The ball fell between two outfielders and rolled by them. By the time they threw it in I was standing on third base and not even breathing very hard. My father gave me a standing ovation. On the other side of the field, Uncle Daddy and Mom were giving each other high fives, too.

I got two more hits that day. The only bad thing that happened was when I tried to steal second. The second baseman was a big kid who stood right next to the base while he was waiting for the throw from the catcher. I tried to slide away from him, but he tagged me and I was out by a mile. Still, it was my best game of the season: three hits, three runs scored, two runs batted in. By the last inning we were leading 15–2. None of them—Mom, Uncle Daddy, my father—left until the final out.

The next day Uncle Daddy took me to his school. I liked working with the janitors. They let me do cool stuff, like climbing up and getting all the balls stuck on the roof. When I got home the phone rang. It was my father.

"Nice game last night," he said. "You've got a nice level swing. You really know how to make contact."

"Thanks."

"You know, that kid blocked second base last night," he said. "That's why you got tagged out."

"Yeah, I know."

"Don't let him do that," my father said. "You've got as much right to that base as he does. I know he's a big kid, but so what? Next time anyone tries to stand between you and the base, you go in high and knock him on his butt, okay?"

"Okay."

"I'm serious," he said. "You do that and I guarantee he won't try that again."

That night I lay in bed thinking about my father's advice. *Go in high and knock him on his butt.* I knew that Uncle Daddy would never say anything like that. Uncle Daddy used words like *cooperate, teamwork, talk it out.*

Two nights later we had another game. Uncle Daddy and Mom and my father were all there, sitting on opposite sides of the field like before. Scott Rothrock was the second baseman on the other team. He was one of the biggest kids in our grade.

"No batter, no batter," Rothrock chanted when I came up to bat in the second inning. He let out a loud whoop after I struck out swinging. I didn't look up when I walked back to the dugout.

In the fourth inning I worked a walk. I waited until the second pitch before I took off to steal second. While I ran I could see Scott Rothrock crouched down waiting for the throw from the catcher. He was doing it, too, standing a good three feet to the first-base side of the bag, expecting me to waste time going the long way around him. This time I ran straight and when I got near second base I barreled into him. I hit him hard on his left side and he grunted and fell and I heard the ball whiz past us into center field. I got up, touched second, and cruised into third base standing up. When I looked up to the bleachers the first thing I saw was my father, standing, pointing straight at me with a huge grin on his face.

That night my father telephoned the house.

"Nice game," he said. "That was some collision at second base. You okay?"

"Yeah," I said, even though my right shoulder did feel sore.

"I'll tell you one thing," my father said. "That kid won't try that with you again."

"Yeah," I said. "Thanks for the tip."

"You're welcome," he said. "With some things you can't go around them. You have to go straight through. Anyway, it's been great coming to your games. I'm going to every one." He paused and then, in a softer voice, he said: "I know I missed some in the past."

"Only about a hundred and fifty." It was a mean thing to say, but it popped out of my mouth and it was true. For a second he didn't say anything.

"Rivers."

"Sorry," I mumbled.

"Rivers, listen to me," he said. "I want to tell you why I was gone for such a long time. I want you to know. Let's meet tomorrow morning and talk."

My first thought was that I didn't want to hear about it, not then, not ever. I tried to swallow but my throat was bone-dry.

13. LOST AND FOUND

My father met me at my house. He called first to clear it with Mom, and showed up at exactly ten o'clock.

"How about we talk in the kitchen," he said.

We sat at the table. I expected him to start right in, but for a whole minute he said nothing. Maybe in the back of my head I was still hoping for one of those simple explanations like you get in a movie. *I had a car accident that gave me a serious case of amnesia. I had to go undercover for the FBI. I got kidnapped by aliens.*

"Have you ever felt claustrophobic?" he asked. "You know what that word means?"

"Yeah," I said. One time I was crawling in a

pipe under the road. I was with Jessie. It was dark and tight in there. Halfway through I started to freak. I wanted to turn back, but Jessie was behind me yelling, and I had to keep going.

"Well, I'd been getting that panicky feeling," he said. "Whenever I would come home from work and saw our house, this house, I'd get that feeling. Like my life was a shirt two sizes too small at the neck. It felt like the walls were closing in. I thought I could handle it, but that feeling kept getting stronger and stronger."

He looked down at his hands. *My father's hands*, I was thinking.

"First I didn't have a care in the world, you know. But all of a sudden I had a house, wife, kid, job, lawn mower. I had all these responsibilities." He gave me a little smile. "Look, you're not supposed to understand any of this, but anyway that's how I felt."

Just then the refrigerator motor turned on and started humming. He leaned forward.

"That's what happened the night I went out to get that pizza," he said. "I paid for it, but when I drove back to our street and saw our little house on our little street with two houses on either side, well, the panic hit so hard I could barely breathe. I made a U-turn and started driving. I drove all night and I could feel that panicky feeling chasing behind me the whole way. In the morning I pulled the car over, slept a couple of hours, and kept driving. I drove all the way to California. Twenty-five hundred miles."

My father kept on talking, but I was thinking of all the states and their capitals between here and California. We studied them in Ms. Vitkevich's class. Iowa: Des Moines. Kansas: Topeka. Nevada: Carson City.

"Did you hear what I just said?" he asked.

"Sorry," I mumbled.

My father said: "I got into trouble with drugs."

"Drugs?" The word sounded ugly when I said it.

"That's what I said." He spread his fingers and spoke to his hands. "Here's what happened. I was in Alaska, working on a fishing boat. Real good money but backbreaking work, eighteen-hour days. No matter how much coffee I drank I couldn't stay awake. One night one of the guys on the crew gave me a pill. Speed. Dexedrine. I took it and it woke me up. I got through that shift. Next night I took another one. Bingo: I'm awake. I thought it was a miracle. All of a sudden I could make myself alert when I needed to. When we got back to port I found a doctor who wrote me a prescription for the stuff. That's how I got started. Pretty stupid, huh?"

That didn't seem to deserve an answer, but I nodded anyway.

"It wasn't too bad at first," he said. "But pretty soon I was taking stronger doses, and the stuff got me so jacked up I had to take another pill—Valium, a downer—to calm me enough so I could sleep." He let out a breath. "I was hooked on pills, uppers and downers, for almost five years. Lost years."

I sat there, breathing.

"There's more to it," he said, "but that's enough for now. Unless you want to ask me anything."

I had a million things I wanted to ask, but all I said was: "Why did you stop taking drugs?"

"One night I took two hits of speed," he said, "and my heart started going crazy, hammering, banging, racing. I called 911, and they took me to the emergency room. At the hospital, there was a guy in the bed next to me who looked like a skeleton. I mean, this guy had almost no meat on him. You could see his bones sticking out of his skin, his eyes bugged out of their sockets. The doctor saw me staring at this guy. 'Take a real good look,' he said, 'because that's going to be you in a few years.' I was sick, real sick, but I didn't want to die."

I sat there, paralyzed.

"I wanted to come home, but I didn't want to come back so long as I was addicted to those pills," he said. "I promised myself that I wouldn't come back to you and your mother until I'd stopped taking pills for at least a year. The first few times I couldn't make it more than two or three months."

He swiveled around so he could face me. "That's not an excuse, Rivers. There's no excuse for what I did. But it's the truth."

Just then Mom walked in. My father stood up.

"Hello," she said.

"I'm on the way out," my father said. He took a deep breath and looked at me. "I'll see you tomorrow night at your game."

He closed the door behind him.

"What was that about?" she asked.

"Nothing," I said.

"Nothing?"

"He told me about why he left and everything," I said.

Mom slid next to me. She tried to give me a hug but I didn't hug back. I felt numb.

"He was addicted to pills," I said.

"I know," she said. "But he says he's been clean for over a year now."

"Do you believe him?" I asked.

"I do," she said. "But I do feel bitter about it. I can't help it. He got on his little roller coaster of pills and amphetamines, and I lost six years of my life."

She looked at me.

"Well, maybe that's not fair," she said. "Your father and I didn't have the greatest marriage in the world. Since he left I've had six years to find out who I am. I'm a whole different person now."

"Where's Uncle Daddy?" I asked Mom. I really needed to talk to him.

"He's going to be staying at school late tonight," Mom said.

The phone rang. It was Taylor.

"Hiya," she said. "What's up?"

"I don't know," I said. "Hey, can you see me now?"

"No," she said, "but I can hear you loud and clear."

"Very funny," I said. "Meet me you-know-where."

"Okay," she said, "but I've got to go to my grandmother's house. I can't meet you till after supper, say around seven."

"Oh, all right," I said. "See you at seven."

14.
THE TALLEST TREE

I headed for the park. Taylor and I had a special tree, a secret place that only we knew about. It was the biggest and tallest tree around, with plenty of branches spaced out for easy climbing. But the best thing was at the top, where eight branches grew close together to make a natural crow's nest. You could sit up there like a lookout at the top of a ship's mast, and no one down below would have a clue you were up there.

My hands were smeared with sticky pine pitch by the time I made it to the top. I'd just gotten settled when I felt the tree shaking down below.

"You're late!" I called down to Taylor, even though I couldn't see her through the green pine needles. A minute later she climbed, grunting, into the crow's nest beside me.

"You know what I like best about this place?" she asked.

"What?"

"It's so far up even the mosquitoes can't find you."

At first we just sat there, saying nothing. I loved being up so high I could look down on all the shorter trees. The sun was beginning to set, and only the treetops were bathed in light. Taylor stretched out her legs.

"This may be my all-time favorite place," she said.

"Me, too. From up here it looks like you could walk on top of the other trees."

"Don't try it," Taylor advised. "Hey, I'm going to camp tomorrow."

"Yeah."

"Wish you were coming, too?"

"Not really," I said, trying to sound casual. But I did feel jealous. The idea of going away for a month sounded terrific.

"Camp is cool," Taylor said, "except for the food. Did I tell you about the time we opened a bag of pizza mix and it had all these bugs in it?"

"Only about ten times," I said.

"I'm hungry," she said. "You want to go to the ice-cream shop?"

"But we just got here."

"I know," she said. "But it may be the last edible food I'll have for the next thirty days."

"My father took me there," I said. "I ordered vanilla."

"But you hate vanilla!" Taylor said.

"I was mad at him," I explained.

"It must be so weird having him back. I mean, you didn't have a father around for so many . . . "

"Hey, don't forget Uncle Daddy," I interrupted.

"Well, okay, but you know what I mean," she said. "And then your father just drops out of the sky. Like, I'm home!"

I needed to tell her what he had told me that morning, but I didn't see an easy way to get it into the conversation. Two birds flew by, skimming over the trees. We watched them fly by. For a long moment neither one of us said anything.

"You know what's the weirdest thing?" I said. "I don't know what to call him. I can't call him Dad."

"How about Father?" she suggested. "How about Papa? Or Pa?"

"See what I mean?" I said. "They all sound completely stupid."

"What *do* you call him?" she asked.

"Nothing."

"Does he come by much?"

"He came by one day," I said. "He brought his toolbox and he went around the house repairing a bunch of things. Uncle Daddy and Mom weren't thrilled about that. Now he mostly calls."

"Repairing stuff?" Taylor asked. "That's a little . . . strange, isn't it? He went away and didn't talk to you guys once in six years. I mean, how's he going to fix that?"

"That's the thing," I said. "He can't."

"Why *did* he leave?" she asked. "Has he ever told you?"

"He told me today," I said, swallowing.

"Well?"

"He got hooked on pills," I said.

"What kind of pills?"

"Uppers. You know, like speed."

"You mean like drugs," she said.

"Yeah." I nodded. "Drugs."

"Did he start taking pills while he was still living with you?" she asked.

"No, after he left."

"But why did he leave? Did he explain that?"

"He said some stuff about it," I said. "He said he was feeling claustrophobic."

"Claustrophobic!" she said in disbelief. "That's still no reason to leave your family for six years."

A breeze blew up. It made a soft hissing sound in the trees. The air smelled fresh and piney. The sky had turned a deep-blue color. Taylor reached around to finger a place where she and I had carved our initials into the bark about a year ago. The scars had healed over but you could still make out the letters.

"How could he walk out like that when you were just a little boy?" Taylor said softly. "I mean, he was your father."

My eyes welled up with tears, and I had to turn away so she wouldn't notice.

"Let's go get a sundae," I said. My throat was tight, and I had to work to make my voice sound right.

We climbed down and walked to the ice-cream shop for sundaes. A half hour later we went to the street corner and said good-bye.

"Wish me luck!" Taylor started crossing the street, but halfway across she stopped, reached down, and picked up something. She brought it back to me.

"Here," she said, smiling. It was a small blue feather. She looked both ways and darted back across the street. I stood there holding the feather, thinking maybe Uncle Daddy would put it in his fat dictionary, and feeling sad that I wouldn't be seeing Taylor for a whole month. I could hear a siren off in the distance. As I turned down my street I heard the siren again, louder this time. Tires squealed, and an ambulance sped past, lights flashing.

"No!" I cried.

The word jumped out of my mouth because the ambulance was heading straight for my house.

15.
CRISIS

I dropped the feather and ran down the street. I could see the ambulance pull into our driveway and lurch to a stop. Four medics jumped out and rushed up the steps into the house. I came charging right behind. As soon as I got inside the living room I saw him lying on the couch.

Uncle Daddy!

The medics were hovering around him, opening his shirt, checking his pulse and breathing. I ran over to him. His eyes were closed, but when I took his hand he gave me a good, hard squeeze.

"Rivers," he said in a weak voice. "Elephant."

"What?" I asked him.

"Stand back, son!" one man said, and I had to back away. I looked up at Mom. She was crying.

"He collapsed about fifteen minutes ago," she told me. "He was in terrible pain. He could barely talk." She looked at one of the medics. "What is . . ."

"Heart," the man told Mom, putting an oxygen mask over Uncle Daddy's face. The word made her gasp.

"What's going on?" someone said. I turned and saw my father. He stared, first at Uncle Daddy, then at Mom, then at me. "I dropped in—" he began.

"We've got to get him to the hospital. Now!" one medic yelled.

They lifted Uncle Daddy enough so they could slide a stretcher under him.

"I'm going with him in the ambulance!" Mom said.

"Me, too!" I cried.

"There's only room for one," the medic told Mom.

"But—" I began.

"Up!" the medic yelled, and they lifted Uncle Daddy.

"I'll drive him," my father offered, looking at Mom.

I ran down the driveway and got into the passenger seat of his VW Bug. In the ambulance, the flashing lights went on and the siren started blaring.

"Hang on," he said, and we sped off, close behind the ambulance. He raced down the streets, squealing around turns, pulling me toward him or flattening me against the door. When the ambulance sailed through a red light he looked left and right and followed behind.

Neither one of us said a word, not even when we got to the hospital and he pulled up right behind the ambulance and I jumped out.

Mom and I rode the elevator to the eighth floor: Intensive Care.

"It's a heart attack," Dr. Harmon, the cardiologist, told Mom. The doctor was young, and she looked like she needed about twelve hours' sleep. "A classic coronary thrombosis. We're trying everything we can to stabilize his condition."

"Stabilize his condition?" Mom snapped. "What is that supposed to mean?"

"It means his condition is very serious," Dr. Harmon said. "His heart is weak. He's got major blockage in two of his arteries. He needs emergency surgery."

"Now?" Mom asked. "But he just had a heart attack."

"As soon as possible," Dr. Harmon said. "We're assembling a team right now. If we can stabilize his condition we'll do the operation at six-thirty tomorrow morning."

Mom swore.

"I'm sorry," she said. "I . . ."

"It's all right," the doctor replied.

"Just tell me he's going to be all right," Mom whispered, starting to cry. "Tell me, please."

I went over to the window. The glass felt cool against my forehead. Down below I could see the hospital parking lot and the yellow VW Bug.

"Why don't you go home?" Dr. Harmon suggested. "He's sleeping now. I promise we'll call you the moment his condition changes."

The doctor wrote down our phone number, and we left.

In the parking lot, the door of the VW Bug opened and my father climbed out. Mom whirled around so her back was to him.

"I'm going to stay," Mom said. "I can't leave him, Rivers. My uncle was always there for me when I needed him. I won't leave him now. Go home with your father."

"But I want to stay, too."

"No," she said. "Go home and get some sleep."

"It's not fair!" I told her.

"I know," she said. She put her hand on my shoulder. "I want you to do this for me, please."

I said nothing.

"Would you stay with Rivers?" she asked my father. "I might be here all night and I don't want him to be alone."

"I'll sleep on the couch," he said.

"Thanks," Mom said to him. She turned to

me. "I'll call you as soon as there's some news." She kissed me and headed back inside.

"What's wrong with him?" my father asked.

"A heart attack," I said, trying not to cry. "He needs an operation."

All of a sudden I felt numb, like I couldn't say another word about it. Maybe he sensed that, because he didn't ask any more questions.

Back home he looked awkward standing in the middle of the room now that he wasn't holding any tools, like he didn't know what to do with his hands. I went to the linen closet, dug out a sheet and blanket, and put them on the sofa.

"I'm going to take a shower," he said.

"Okay," I said. I went back to the linen closet to get him a clean towel. Then I went into the kitchen and poured a bowl of cereal. I sat there in that quiet kitchen, noticing Uncle Daddy's stuff all over the place. His keys hanging next to the refrigerator. His fishing cap on its hook. His extra-bran cereal. His vitamins on the counter.

I finished my cereal and plopped my bowl into the sink. On the way to my bedroom I spotted a sweatshirt Uncle Daddy had left balled up on the living-room couch. I picked it up and pushed my nose into it. The sweatshirt smelled so much like him that I started to cry. I tried to stop but I couldn't, and I pressed the cloth over my mouth to muffle the sound.

16.
THE WAITING GAME

A loud clanging sound woke me up. I followed the sound to the laundry room. My father was working on some pipes behind the washing machine.

"Morning," he said.

"Did Mom call?" I asked him.

He nodded.

"She's going to call back in half an hour," he told me. "Hey, you hungry?"

"I guess."

"I made some bacon," he said. "C'mon. I'll fry you some eggs to go with it."

A few minutes later I was devouring a plate of

bacon, eggs, and buttery toast. He sipped coffee and watched me eat.

"You used to help me eat my breakfast," he said, smiling. "You'd climb up on my lap and I'd give you pieces of toast and you'd dip them into the yolk."

I couldn't remember that. The phone rang, and I jumped to answer it.

"Hi, Rivers." It was Mom.

"How is Uncle Daddy?"

"Well, they didn't do the operation," she said. "He's still too weak. The doctor said maybe later today. Are you okay?"

"Yeah."

"You sure?"

"I'm sure," I said.

"I'll call you as soon as I know something," she said and hung up.

I was driving myself crazy. I couldn't read, I couldn't watch TV, I couldn't do anything. Finally I told my father I was going out for a walk.

"Want company?" he asked.

"No, that's okay."

"I'll be here," he said.

I went down to the park, but it was deserted. Someone had left a basketball, and I tried to shoot baskets, but the ball was too dead to dribble, so I gave up and walked into the woods.

I headed straight for the big tree. Usually it was real breezy up there, but today when I reached the top it was perfectly still. Like time had stopped. I sat in the crow's nest looking up at the sky. I wished I could climb higher—first to the clouds, then the moon, the planets, the stars. I didn't want to come down, ever.

I kept thinking about Uncle Daddy. When I was about four, I was terrified of getting a shot, but Uncle Daddy played a game to help me get through it. He'd put me in his lap and put his face close to mine, so we were practically eyeball to eyeball, and together we'd say:

Iddle dit and iddle dit
and iskiddlie ote and dote
and bobo skeedeet and dat
and walla kachew!

It was just nonsense but we kept saying those words, over and over, giggling and laughing, and when the doctor stuck the needle in my arm I hardly noticed.

When I got back home, my father had moved the washing machine to the middle of the kitchen floor.

"Look at this," my father said. He pointed to the floor in the laundry room. "The wood's all rotted out. I'm going to replace the floor." He looked at me. "Your mother called ten minutes ago. His condition is still the same."

"I want to see him," I said.

"She didn't say anything about visiting hours."

"I don't care," I said. "I've got to see him."

"All right, then," he said, nodding at me. "Give me a minute to wash up."

Mom seemed surprised to see me in the Intensive Care Waiting Room.

"What are you doing here?" she asked.

"I have to see him," I said. "I have to."

"Well, let me go ask the nurse," she said.

A minute later she came back.

"Must be your lucky day," she said. "You can see him. But just for a few minutes."

The room was small. He was lying on the bed, staring up at a tiny TV. Above him two bags of medicine dripped something into his arm. When the door closed he turned and smiled.

"Rivers," he said weakly. He hit the remote to turn off the TV.

"Hi, Uncle Daddy." I moved to the side of his bed.

"How are you doing?" he asked.

"Okay."

"You look worried."

I nodded, looking down.

"Hey, I'm a tough old bird," he said. "Just ask the doctor. How do I look?"

"You look okay," I lied. His face looked awful—old and tired and all washed out. Even his voice sounded different. "This place smells like medicine. The nasty kind."

"I'll be home to watch you play baseball before you know it," he said.

"Yeah," I said. Playing baseball was about the last thing I felt like doing. "You know when the medics came to the house? You said the word *elephant* to me. What did you mean?"

"Oh yes," Uncle Daddy said. He closed his eyes. "When I first got that pain it felt like I had a full-grown elephant standing on my chest. I couldn't breathe."

I felt so scared. What I wanted more than anything was for him to take care of me. To tell me a story like he used to do when I was little. A story with a happy ending.

"My body tried to warn me about this, but I didn't listen." Uncle Daddy started coughing, trying to clear his throat.

"Don't," I said.

He pointed to a pitcher of water on the table by the bed. Uncle Daddy coughed harder, his face getting red. I looked all around the room but I couldn't find a glass, not even one lousy cup. What kind of cheap hospital was this anyway? I started to panic. Where was Mom? Where were the nurses?

Suddenly I knew what to do. I dipped my hand into the pitcher. The water was colder than I expected. I cupped some water in my hand and brought it to Uncle Daddy's mouth. He drank from my hand. Some water dripped down onto his shirt, but he ignored it and drank and his coughing stopped.

I brought more water to his mouth but my hands started shaking. More water fell onto his shirt. I could see he was getting drenched but he didn't seem to care. He took another swallow from my hand-cup and looked at me, and I didn't realize I was crying until he reached out and pulled me against his wet shirt. "I'm going to be okay, Rivers. Trust me on this one. I'm going to be okay."

17. WILDFLOWERS

I had lunch with Mom and hung around the hospital another hour, but I was driving myself crazy. Finally I called my father to pick me up. On the way home I asked him to drop me off at the park. There was one kid sitting on a swing. Ethan Pierce.

"Hey, Ethan!" I said, taking the swing next to his. I was actually sort of glad to see him.

"I heard about your uncle," he said. "That's too bad. He's real sick, huh?"

"I guess," I told him. "He had a heart attack."

"You know my mom's friend, the one who works at his school?" Ethan asked. "Well, she came to the house, and I heard her and my mom talking about it. She told my mother that people at the school are making plans for . . . you know . . ." His voice trailed off.

"For what?" I asked.

"Maybe I shouldn't have said anything," he said, getting off the swing.

"What are you talking about?" I demanded.

"Okay, you asked," he said. He took a deep breath. "They said the school is making plans for the funeral."

I blinked at him.

"There's just one problem with that," I said. "He's not dead."

"I know, I know. But I guess they want to be ready," Ethan said with a shrug. "The whole school is going to come to the church. All the kids are going to get dressed up and they're all going to carry wildflowers. Your uncle likes wildflowers, right?"

"You're kidding," I said. This was one of Ethan's pranks. It had to be. Then it hit me: he wasn't joking.

"You better shut up," I said evenly.

"Maybe I shouldn't have said anything," Ethan said.

"You've got some nerve," I said, taking a step toward him. "They're going to operate on him tonight."

"Hey, that's good," he said, moving back.

"They're going to operate on him," I said again. "Tonight."

"I hope he gets better," Ethan said. "Really. Listen, this wasn't my idea. I'm just telling you what I heard. Hey, I better go! See you!"

I stared as he ran away.

I walked home, thinking hard. I knew that what Ethan had told me was true, every word of it, and the only way to describe my mood would be with a word I'd just learned: flabbergasted. I came through a field, and I was wearing shorts, so I could feel the wildflowers brushing against my legs, the kind Uncle Daddy loved, daisies and Queen Anne's lace, buttercups, and clover. At the edge of the field a whole pack of black-eyed Susans stared as I hiked past.

My father barbecued steaks for dinner. We ate at the picnic table while the sun slipped behind the trees. I didn't think I was hungry, and I was almost embarrassed at how much I ate and how good it tasted.

"Meat okay?" he asked.

"Mmmm," I said. Out of the corner of my eye I watched the way he ate, forking together baked potato, corn, and meat in one megabite. Exactly how I ate.

The phone rang, and I ran inside to answer it.

"It's me," Mom said. "They're bringing him into surgery."

"Surgery," I repeated. "That's good, right?"

"It's still touch-and-go," Mom said. "The surgeon told me she's 'cautiously optimistic,' whatever that means. We won't know anything until later. I'll let you know. . . ."

For a moment neither one of us said anything.

"Pray for him, Rivers," she whispered. "Pray."

"I will, I will," I whispered back.

After supper I went to the living room and dropped onto the couch. My father saw me staring at the blank TV.

"Works even better if you turn it on," he commented.

"Do you remember that kid you met at the ice-cream store?" I asked. "Ethan Pierce? I saw him at the park today and he got me so mad. He was saying that the teachers at the school are planning Uncle Daddy's funeral. All the kids from the school are going to bring wildflowers to the church. I'm like: *There's just one problem. He's not exactly dead.* Can you believe that? He's such a jerk!"

"Well, you heard what your mother said," my father replied. "It's touch-and-go. I mean, it could happen."

"No way," I said, shaking my head. "No possible way."

He sat back, looking at me.

"He's not going to die," I said and I thought: *If he does, you think you can move in here and take his place. Well, you better think again.*

"He's been real good to you both," he said softly.

I couldn't make myself look at him, so I snapped on the TV and turned up the volume.

Pray, Mom had said. But I felt too mad to pray.

I watched TV until my eyes got tired, but I still didn't feel like going to bed.

As a little kid I always knew there was a big warm spot for me in Uncle Daddy's chest. Hundreds and thousands of times I had run to him and pressed myself against that place while he folded me into a hug. Now the surgeon would cut open his chest to try to fix the heart beating inside.

I was *so* scared.

In Uncle Daddy's room I found his bathrobe in the closet, pulled it off the hook, and slipped my arms into the sleeves. When I went back to the couch I felt safe, wrapped in the warm cocoon of that robe and Uncle Daddy's good smell. My father smiled when he saw me.

"It's a tad big for you, don't you think?" he asked.

"Nope," I told him.

At ten o'clock my father went to the bathroom to wash up. By then I could barely keep my eyes open, so I crawled into my bed, still wearing Uncle Daddy's bathrobe. But when I closed my eyes all I could see were all those kids from Uncle Daddy's school walking single-file into church. I could picture them marching in with those wildflowers, each one carrying a bouquet of clover. I hated Ethan Pierce for telling me that, because I couldn't find any way to get that picture out of my head.

I must have fallen asleep, because I suddenly felt someone trying to wake me. I opened my eyes and saw Mom. She was sobbing in a terrible choking way, and I knew the worst thing in the world had just happened, but at first I couldn't understand the gush of words pouring out of her mouth.

"He's going to be all right, Rivers! He's going to live! He's going to live!"

18. THE HEART, REBUILT

It was after 9 A.M. when I finally woke up. I smelled bacon again and it got my stomach rumbling. My father was in the kitchen, drinking coffee and reading the paper.

"Morning," he said with a smile. "That's great news about your great-uncle."

"I know." I couldn't help smiling back.

"Hey, you want some breakfast?" he asked. "Bacon and eggs, just like yesterday?"

"Okay," I said. "Don't you have to go to work?"

"I'm taking a couple days off."

He took three eggs out of the refrigerator

and started juggling them. He juggled them for a full minute before he caught them, *one, two, three.*

"Pretty nifty, huh? I bet for a second you were wondering if you'd be eating scrambled eggs! It's not as easy as it looks, but I can teach you. You want me to?"

"Maybe," I said.

"Great," he said, cracking eggs into the hot pan. Mom came into the kitchen just as I was mopping up the yolk with my toast crusts.

"Good morning," he said.

"It sure is," she said, sitting down at the table. "I smell coffee. I hope it's strong."

He poured her some coffee and then poured more for himself. I noticed that my father stayed standing while he sipped from his mug.

Mom told us what she knew about Uncle Daddy's condition.

"The doctor said the recovery will take at least a month, probably two," she said. "I think we've got enough money to hire a part-time nurse, but it's still going to be extra work. We'll have to haul stuff up to his bedroom and down the stairs."

My father walked over to the door between the kitchen and the garage.

"Come here," he said to Mom. She got up and stood by him. He opened the door and pointed into the garage. I came over to look, too. "What about this room right here?"

Mom looked, first at the garage, then at him.

"What room?" she asked.

"Here." He opened the door and walked until he was standing inside the garage on the right-hand side. He turned to face us, and used his hands to make a big rectangle in the air. "This is the door, right here, so you can enter through the garage. Okay? Over here is a nice big window that looks out on the lawn. There's a smaller window over here, and you've already got that door for easy access from the kitchen. Can you see it?"

I could see Mom thinking.

"We never use this part of the garage anyway," she said. "How long would it take to build it?"

"When is he coming home from the hospital?" he asked back.

"Three weeks," she said. "He has to go to some kind of heart rehab first."

"Well, three weeks, then," he said.

"Can you really do it that fast?" she asked him.

"It'll be tight but we can do it," he said. "I know a guy who would help out with the heavy work."

"Let's do it, Mom!" I said. "It would be perfect for Uncle Daddy."

Mom stood there, looking at the empty garage.

"I would feel better having him near the kitchen where we can keep a close watch on him," she said. She looked at my father. "How much would it cost?"

"Nothing for the labor," he said softly. "Just materials. And I'd have to pay the guy to help."

"Okay," Mom said after a moment. "Let's do it!" She looked at me. "We'll keep this a secret from Uncle Daddy."

"When can I see him?" I asked.

"The doctor said we might be able to see him this afternoon," Mom said.

"You've got a few hours to kill," my father said to me. "What do you say we take a trip to the lumber yard?"

• • •

At four o'clock we went to the hospital. Uncle Daddy was still pretty groggy from the drugs they gave him during the operation. Mom had told me that he looked bad—like "death warmed over" is how she put it—and I was glad she'd warned me.

"Hey, Uncle Daddy!" I ran over to his bed.

"Rivers, Rivers." He smiled and reached for my hand. "The rivers are flowing, Rivers."

"Huh?"

"My blood," he said. "The surgeon unclogged my arteries, bless her heart. Guess I look pretty bad."

"You look wonderful," Mom told him. She gave me a hard look. "Doesn't he?"

"You bet," I agreed.

"C'mon, you two can lie better than that," he said.

We didn't stay long. But next morning we came back for a second visit, and this time he looked ten times better. He sat up in bed and sipped from a cup while we chatted.

"What's going on at home?" he asked.

"You won't believe this," I said. I told him about my talk with Ethan Pierce at the park, and all the plans for Uncle Daddy's funeral.

"Isn't that awful?" Mom said. But Uncle Daddy was beaming.

"Are you kidding?" he asked. "It's wonderful! I say, let's do it!"

"What?" Mom and I looked at each other.

"I want my students to bring me those wildflowers," he said slowly. "Here. At the hospital."

"You really . . . want them to do that?" Mom asked him.

"I sure do!" he said.

"But, Uncle Dan, I don't think they'd let them do it," Mom said. "I mean, they'd be breaking a thousand hospital rules and regulations."

"I'm a school principal," Uncle Daddy reminded her. "In my world I make the rules and regulations!"

"This isn't your school," she reminded him.

"Just watch," Uncle Daddy replied with a grin.

That day Uncle Daddy made a phone call. Mom came home and made a few more calls. It was definitely against the rules, but the hospital agreed to make an exception in this case so long as Dr. Harmon agreed. We were there the next day when she came into Uncle Daddy's hospital room.

"I'm worried about your strength, your stamina," she told him. "You've just been through major surgery. Talking to a bunch of kids will be exhausting. It might set back your recovery."

"I'll take my chances," Uncle Daddy said, folding his arms.

"I'm sorry," the doctor said. "I don't recommend it."

Uncle Daddy sat up in bed and gave her a straight look.

"If you don't let my students bring me wildflowers," he said, "I'm going to cloud up and rain all over you!"

Dr. Harmon blinked.

"That's my uncle's idea of a joke," Mom explained. "Listen, doctor, I think seeing those kids will help him recover. His students love him. He gets a lot of energy from the children at his school."

Dr. Harmon took a long look at Uncle Daddy.

"All right," she said. "I'll allow it. A *small* number of students. But not for at least four days. And I'm telling you right now that I'm going to be watching very closely. If you start getting tired, I'm going to send those kids home. Is that clear?"

"Aye, aye, Captain!" Uncle Daddy grinned.

Four days later, Uncle Daddy was smiling when we walked into his hospital room. He had on a clean shirt. His hair was combed. A nurse poked her head into the room.

"Ready?" she asked. "The kids are here!"

Dr. Harmon flashed Mom an *I'm not sure this is such a great idea* smile, but at least she was smiling.

A tall girl wearing a white dress entered the room. She was carrying a bouquet of black-eyed Susans.

"I hope you feel better, Mr. Westlake," she said, and gave him the flowers.

"Thanks, Justine," he said.

The next girl came in and kissed Uncle Daddy on the cheek when she gave him her flowers. The one after her was a boy.

"Very thoughtful of you," Uncle Daddy said, looking at the flowers. "Where did you pick them, Darren?"

"My mother picked them for me," the boy admitted.

"Well, tell her for me she has a good eye," Uncle Daddy said.

"Mr. Westlake, could I see your scar?" Darren asked.

"It's under all these bandages," Uncle Daddy said, reaching for his chest.

"No," Dr. Harmon said, shaking her head.

"Sorry, she's the boss," Uncle Daddy told Darren. "But thanks for asking."

"Is your heart better?" one boy asked Uncle Daddy.

"Better than better!" he replied, touching his chest.

"Can the doctor fix your head, too," the boy said, "so you won't be bald?"

That cracked everybody up.

It was just how I pictured it when Ethan Pierce described it, except all the kids' faces were smiling instead of serious. And all those wildflowers. Soon the nurses were taking bunches of flowers away and giving them to other patients.

"How's our big wildflower doing?" the surgeon asked Uncle Daddy. "You look a little wilted."

"Never felt better in my life," Uncle Daddy said. "Now what I really need is some fresh air and sunshine. Think you could arrange that?"

"Easy does it," Dr. Harmon said, smiling. "You'll be home before you know it."

19.
EXTENDED FAMILY

My father hired a man named Derrick to help him turn the garage into a bedroom. Derrick had huge arms, like the arms of a professional wrestler. He'd put a nail into the wood and—BANG—drive it home with a single blow of the hammer. And when it came time to Sheetrock, he lifted the big pieces like they were oversized graham crackers.

I couldn't do much but I kept plenty busy fetching nails, boards, tools, plus helping with the clean-up. Each afternoon I washed my face and hands so I could go see Uncle Daddy at the hospital.

When Derrick left, after the second day, there was still a ton of work to do. My father had to spackle the seams, sand, paint, lay a wood floor, etc. We worked hard, and while we worked we talked. He had plans to help me build a tree house, if I wanted. He wanted to know everything about me—school, friends, grades, sports, hobbies.

But I kept trying to turn the conversation back to him. I had just the outline of those missing years he lived without us. I asked lots of questions.

"What did you do after you left?" I asked.

"Worked," he said. "I took all kinds of jobs."

"Like what?" I asked.

"You name it, I did it," he said. "Bartender, butcher, construction worker, housepainter, carpenter. You wouldn't believe some of the jobs I had. I even washed dishes for a while. Pass me that level."

I handed it to him. He took it, but I didn't move.

"What?" he asked.

"I still don't get it," I said. "Why you never came back."

"I did come back," he said in a low voice. "Once."

"You did?"

"Yeah," he said, nodding. "It was almost exactly two years after I left. I missed you guys so bad I drove all night, six hundred miles, till I got here. I drove in one morning and parked down the street and slouched down in the front seat and waited. I was afraid somebody would call the police on me. And then I saw you come around the house from the back. You couldn't have been more than five, Rivers. You sat down on the front stoop, wearing a cowboy hat and a red shirt."

He slumped back against the unfinished wall and covered his face with his dirty hands.

"I wanted so bad to come running over to my little boy," he said in a soft, high voice. "I wanted to put you on my lap and give you a big hug." He looked at me, mouth trembling. "But I didn't."

"Why not?"

"I wasn't clean," he said. "I was jacked up on

those pills. So I watched you from my car, and then I turned on the engine and drove away."

I was counting the days until Uncle Daddy came home. On the next-to-last day my father installed electrical outlets and a jack for the telephone. On the last day Mom, my father, and I painted the walls, while a man laid carpet on the floor.

"Terrific," Mom said when it was finally finished. "But we can't stop now. We still have to move all his stuff down here, and set up his room, and we've only got three hours to do it."

We hustled upstairs. I brought clothes from the closet while Mom and my father took apart the bed and hauled that down.

"Where should we set up the bed?" she asked.

"Over by the window," I said.

My father nodded. "That's where I'd want it," he agreed.

We took the drawers out of the dresser, but it was still heavy. Mom and my father worked hard trying to carry it down the stairs.

"Will it fit around that corner?" Mom asked. She was breathing hard.

"Piece of cake," he said. "Lift it up and rotate about forty-five degrees."

"Like this?" she asked.

"Perfect." They set the dresser down in the hallway. He looked at her and smiled. "You're pretty strong. Do you go to the gym?"

"I don't need to," she said. "Lifting mailbags at work has given me a real strong back."

"I noticed," he said.

We each must have made twenty trips bringing Uncle Daddy's stuff from his upstairs bedroom down to the new bedroom. We didn't even stop for lunch. I put books in his bookcase while Mom made the bed.

"Looks real homey," Mom said. "Nice job, guys."

"One more thing," my father said. He took a framed photograph of me when I was in first grade, and held it against the wall above the dresser.

"This okay?" he mumbled. It was hard to hear his words because he had nails and picture hooks in his mouth. Mom laughed and moved beside him.

"Are you hungry, Nelson?" she asked in a teasing voice. "Can I get you something to eat? Hmm?"

"Don't get me laughing," he mumbled, "or I'll swallow one of these!"

At the hospital I waited while Mom signed a bunch of papers. Uncle Daddy was all smiles when they brought him down in a wheelchair. Mom and I helped him into the back seat of the car.

"I was starting to wonder if I'd ever get out of that hospital," Uncle Daddy said.

Mom pulled into the garage, and we helped him out of the car. My father came out of the house.

"Welcome back," he said.

Uncle Daddy looked surprised and a little confused to see the new room. I pulled the door all the way open, and beamed at him.

"Son of a gun," he said, looking around.

“Son of a gun. Did you build it?” he asked my father.

“I had help,” my father replied.

We had set up Uncle Daddy’s desk and dresser just like they had been upstairs.

“You guys did one heckuva job.”

“Let’s go in the kitchen,” Mom said. “We’re going to have a little welcome-home party. I even bought a chocolate cake. Low-fat, of course.”

“Well, I’d better run along,” my father said. He started backing up, edging toward the door. He smiled at Uncle Daddy. “I’m real glad you’re on the mend, Dan.”

He gave a little wave as he slipped through the door. Mom and Uncle Daddy exchanged a look. Then Mom looked at me and motioned with her head. I opened the door and stepped outside.

“Where are you going?” I called.

“I’ll catch you later,” he said. “I figure you guys need some time to yourselves.”

“Don’t go,” I said. “Mom set a place for you, Dad.”

The word just slipped out. I think it surprised

me as much as it surprised him. He started to say something and stopped. Then he looked down and blinked.

"Okay, then," he said softly, and followed me inside.

Next morning Mom was in the kitchen, whistling softly, when I walked in. She put her finger to her lips when she saw me.

"He's still sleeping," she whispered. "The doctor said that he'll need a lot of extra sleep."

I poured myself a bowl of cereal.

"I was wondering about you and Dad," I said.

Mom peered at me, waiting.

"Think you two might, you know, get back together?" I asked.

"When he first showed up I would've said no way," she said. "But now . . ." She shrugged. "I don't know."

"You're not mad at him anymore?"

"Mad?" She scratched her head and got up to pour herself some coffee. "I'm not sure that's the word. I am still angry at your father. He walked out on me. On us. But in the last few weeks I learned something, and it surprised me: I still care about him. I still feel married to him." She looked at me. "Are you okay about that?"

"Yeah," I said.

She gave me a questioning look.

"But what about Uncle Daddy?" I said. "I don't want him to leave."

"I know," she said. "And I promise you I'll do everything in my power to keep him here with us."

An hour later I visited Uncle Daddy in his new room. He was lying on his bed, studying an X ray.

"Look at this, Rivers," he said. "My new heart, totally rebuilt. The doctor said there's no reason why it shouldn't run another hundred thousand miles."

He handed me the X ray.

"You should put this in the memory book," I said.

"Good idea! But I can't lift anything heavy right now. Can you get it down for me?"

"I'll try." I climbed up onto a chair and slid

the fat dictionary off the shelf. Then I carried it back to Uncle Daddy.

"Are you going to put it next to *X ray*?" I asked.

"No, we'll put it right here, next to *heart*."

"I told Dad about this book," I said. "He liked the idea, mostly."

"Mostly?"

"He said some memories are too big to fit into a book like this."

Uncle Daddy nodded.

"How's it going between you two?" he asked.

"We're going to build a tree house out back," I said.

"Good," Uncle Daddy said.

"I guess."

"What is it, Rivers?"

"It's hard to explain."

"Try."

"I like spending time with him," I said, "but I don't ever want to stop doing stuff with you."

"I don't want that, either," Uncle Daddy said seriously. "No reason why you can't have a slice of us both."

"This morning I asked Mom if she and Dad would ever . . . get back together," I said. "She said maybe."

"The heart is a mysterious thing," Uncle Daddy said, taking one last look at his X ray before he closed the big book.

"But I don't want you to leave," I told him. "Ever!"

"I'm not going anywhere." He smiled. "You're stuck with me. Here. Think you can lift it back up there?"

"Sure thing." I hoisted the memory book back onto the shelf, and it felt lighter than when I took it down.

A few nights later Dad cooked out on the grill, steaks for him and me, a healthy piece of salmon for Uncle Daddy, and some kind of vegetarian burger for Mom. We had potato salad, corn on the cob, and a big salad to go with it. We sat together at the picnic table.

"How's your salmon?" Dad asked Uncle Daddy.

"*Magnifique!*" he replied, kissing his fingertips.

"That steak smells wonderful," Mom said.

"Have some," Uncle Daddy urged. "It wouldn't kill you, Ana."

"Yeah, Mom," I put in. "Couldn't you just forget you're a vegetarian for one night?"

"It doesn't work that way," she said, laughing. "But it is tempting."

"I have an idea," Uncle Daddy said. "Every year we have an Un-Birthday party for Rivers, right? Well, I was thinking we should do something like that for me. You know, to celebrate the fact that this heart attack didn't kill me. We could call it the Un-Dead party. We could celebrate it every year around this time. What do you think?"

Mom looked horrified.

"You don't think that's a little . . . morbid?" she asked.

We sat there, the four of us, eating and talking. The only weird thing about it was that it didn't feel weird. It felt pretty good and regular. The night had settled in around us, and I could see fireflies blinking on the back lawn. When I was little, fireflies used to scare me. After I got over being scared of them they used to make me sad. I felt sorry for them, the way they wandered through the night shining their tiny flashlights, as if they were looking for something they had lost and would never find. Like me. But tonight they seemed like they had found what they were looking for, or something close to it, and I felt lucky they had chosen our back yard to shine their strange, wild light.

"Hope you saved room for dessert," Mom said. She got up and started clearing the plates. "I made key lime pie."

"Let me help," Dad said. He grabbed some plates and followed her into the kitchen. Uncle Daddy leaned back and looked up.

"Look! You can see the Milky Way." He winked at me. "A river of stars, huh, Rivers?"

"I still wish I had a regular name. Like Tim or Dan."

"Or maybe Ethan," he teased.

"Hey!"

"Rivers," he said. And it sounded all right when he said it. "It's a strong name. I think you'll grow into it."

"I guess."

"Remember when you were little I used to tell you that story about the boy who lived on the river?"

"*Huckleberry Finn,*" I said.

"That's right." He smiled and put his hand on my hand. "Huck and his friend Tom Sawyer had lots of adventures—just like you—but things always turned out okay in the end. You made me tell you those stories over and over. Remember?"

I just looked at him.

As if I could ever forget.